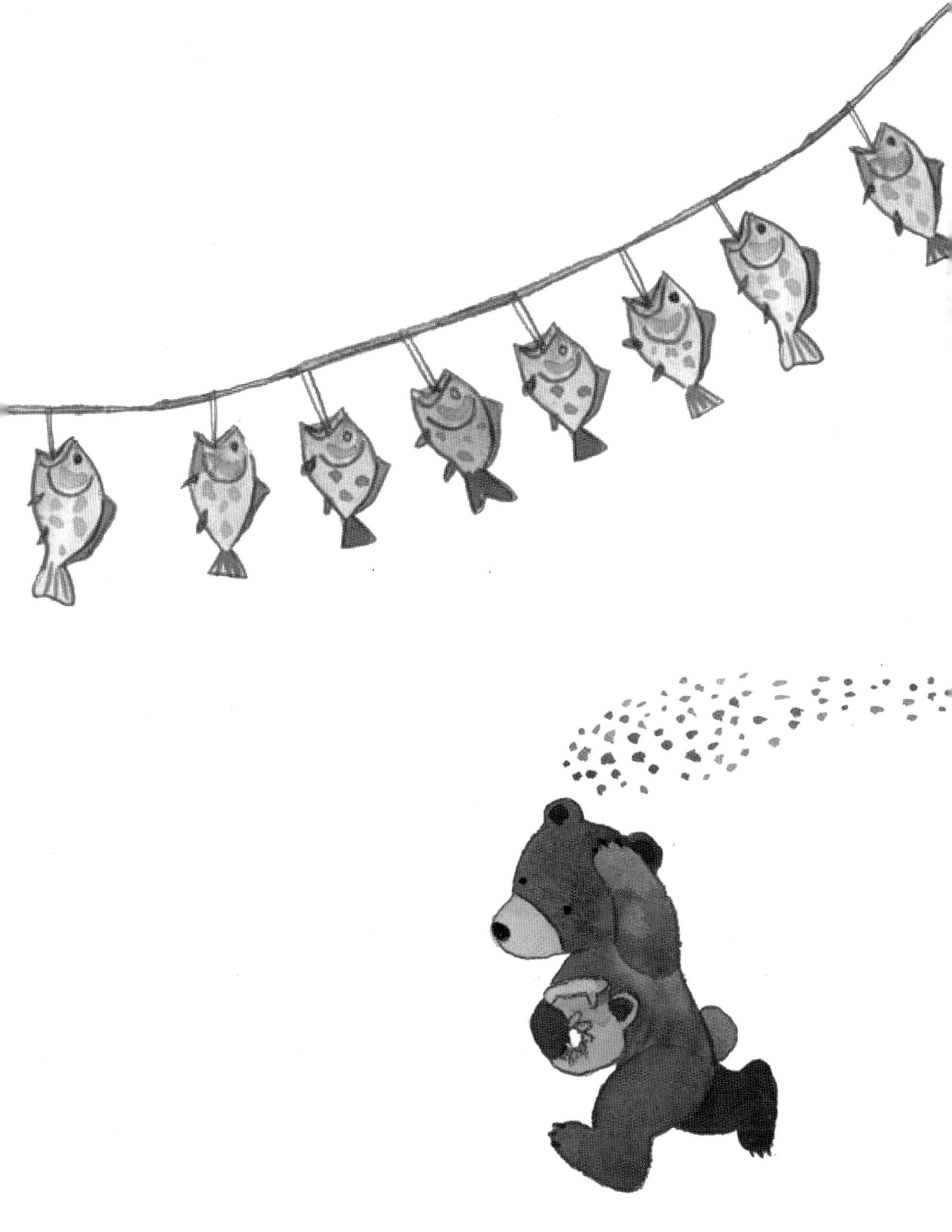

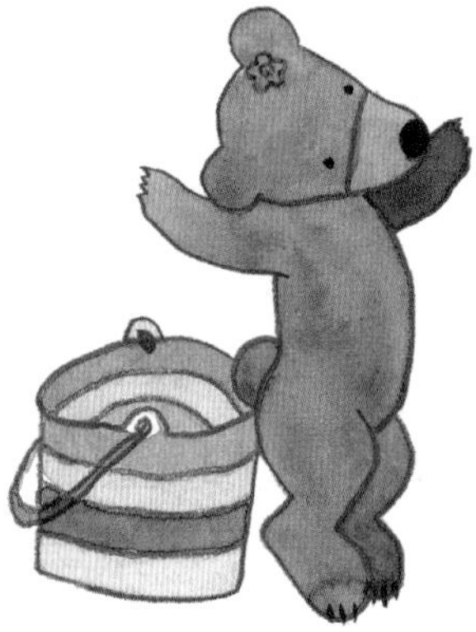

CARDINAL MEDIA

Edited by Denice Jasper

ISBN 978-1-64074-004-4
Through Phoenix Juvenile and Children's Publishing Ltd.

Printed in China
2 4 6 8 10 9 7 5 3 1

Benny Bear
Learns a Lesson

Written by Fang Yuan

Illustrated by Zhu Chengliang

CARDINAL MEDIA

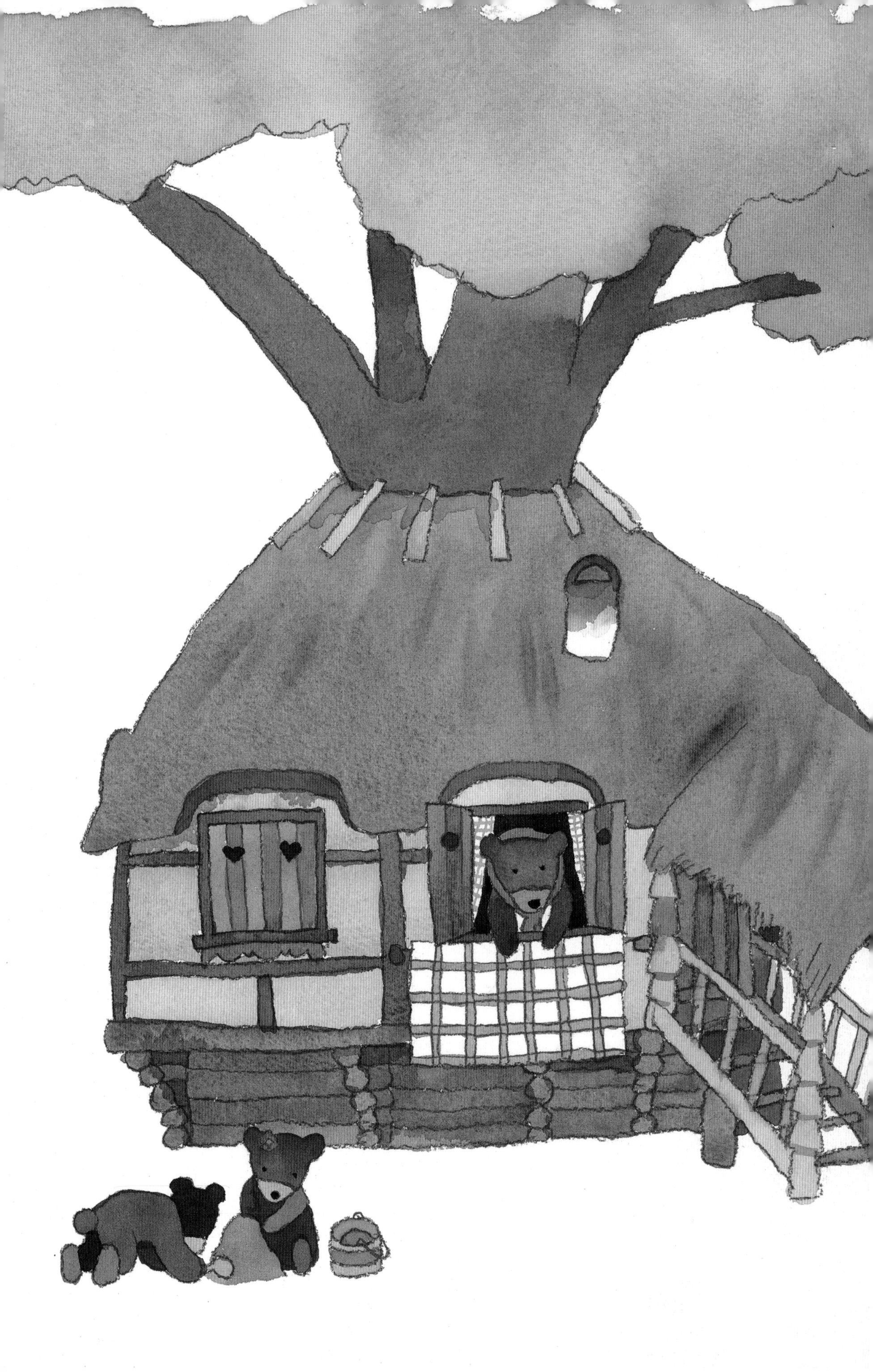

Mother Bear lived with her two little bears, Benny Bear and Lily Bear.

One morning, Benny Bear braved the dangerous bees to scoop out a pot of honey.

Benny Bear brought Mother Bear
the honey and asked her to make
his favorite honey and hazelnut cake.

The cake would take
some time to make,
so the little bears
went outside to play.
Mother Bear said to them,
"Don't go near humans."

Flowers were blossoming in the meadow and Lily Bear made daisy chains to wear. She started to dance.

Benny Bear thought dancing was boring.
He looked for leaves and berries to eat.

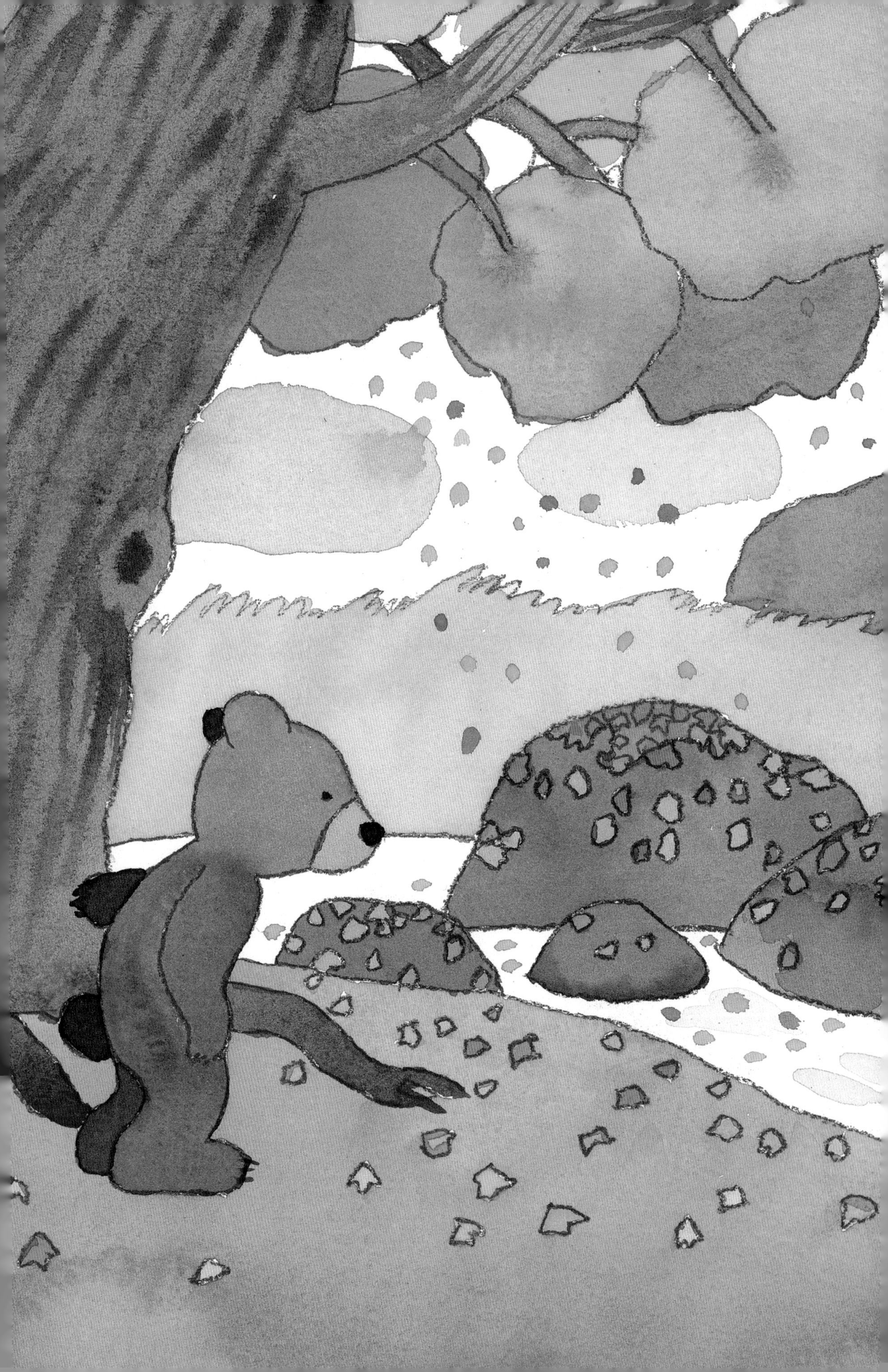

Benny Bear wandered to the stream and spied a fisherman casting a net. Mother Bear had warned him to stay away from humans.

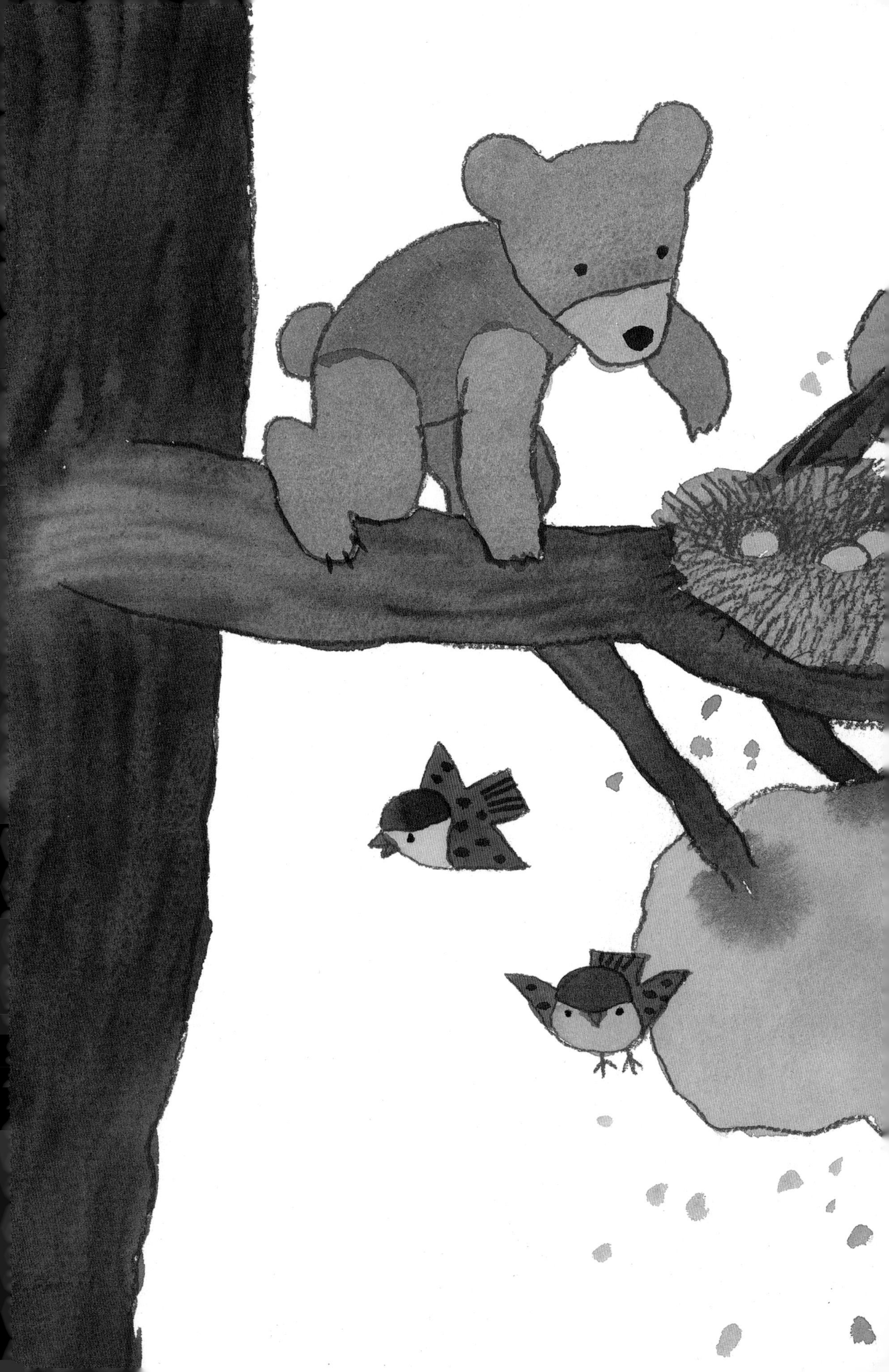

Benny Bear thought he would not get too close if he climbed a tree. He was curious about fishing with a net. Mother Bear did not use a net when she fished.

From the tree, he saw the fisherman's house with many things to explore!

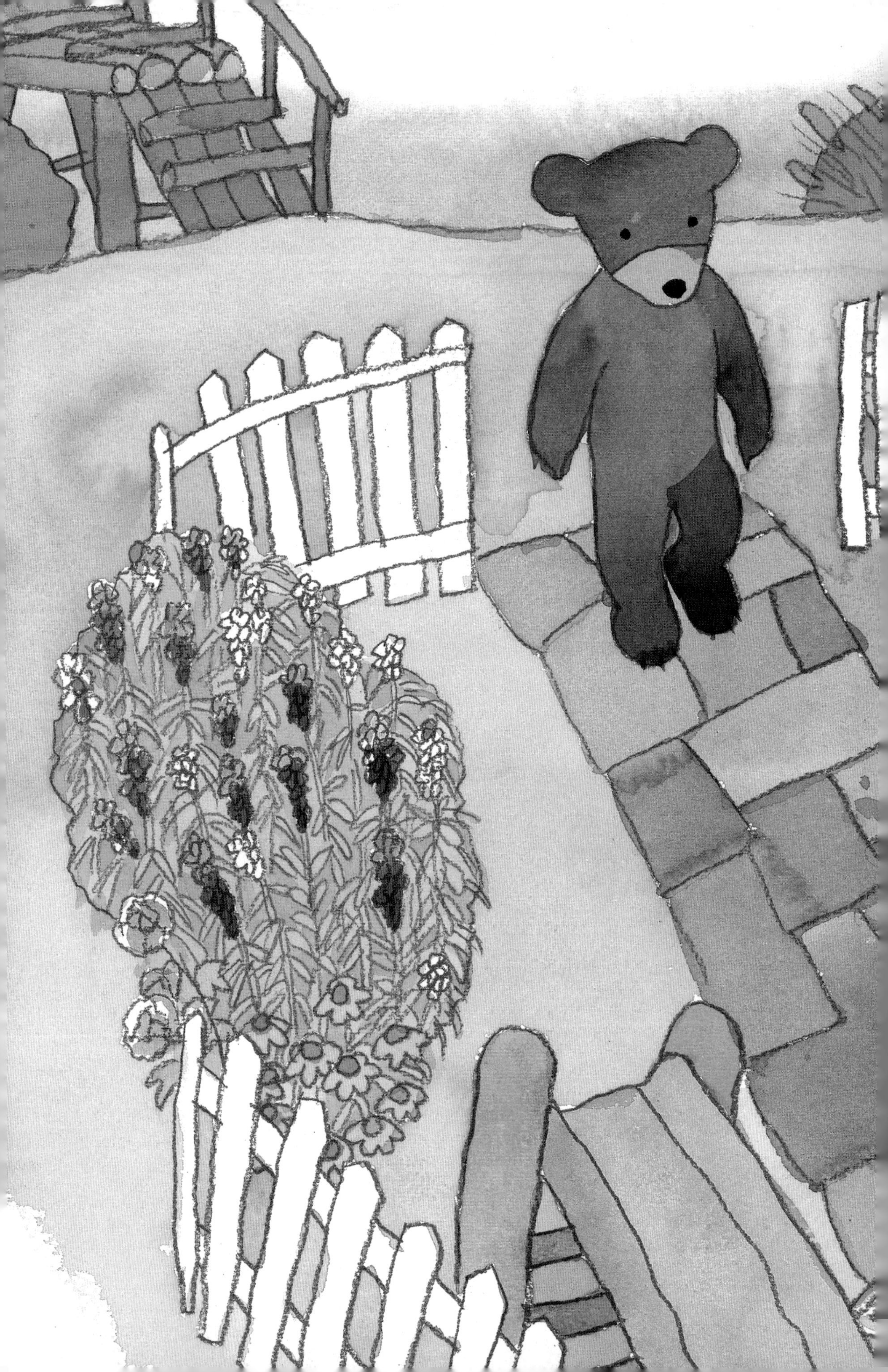

Benny Bear forgot his mother's warning to stay away from humans. He wandered into the fisherman's yard.

Benny Bear began
to explore.

In the backyard, he found something he had never seen. What was that round thing?

Benny Bear climbed onto it and jumped.
He could jump very high. What fun!

Then Benny Bear saw a fishing net. He wanted to see how it worked.

But he got too close and became tangled.

The more Benny Bear tried to free himself, the more tangled he became. He called for help.

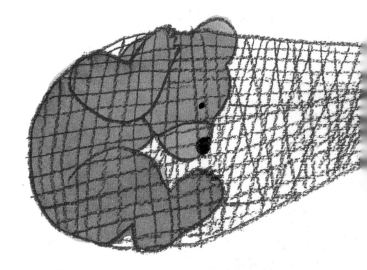

Lily Bear had been looking for her little brother and heard his cry. She tried and tried but could not free him from the net.

Lily Bear ran as fast as she could to get Mother Bear.

Mother Bear came quickly. Together they pulled on the net and freed him.

Mother Bear picked up Benny Bear
and hurried back to the forest.
She was very angry and said,
"I hope you've learned your lesson!
Never go near humans."

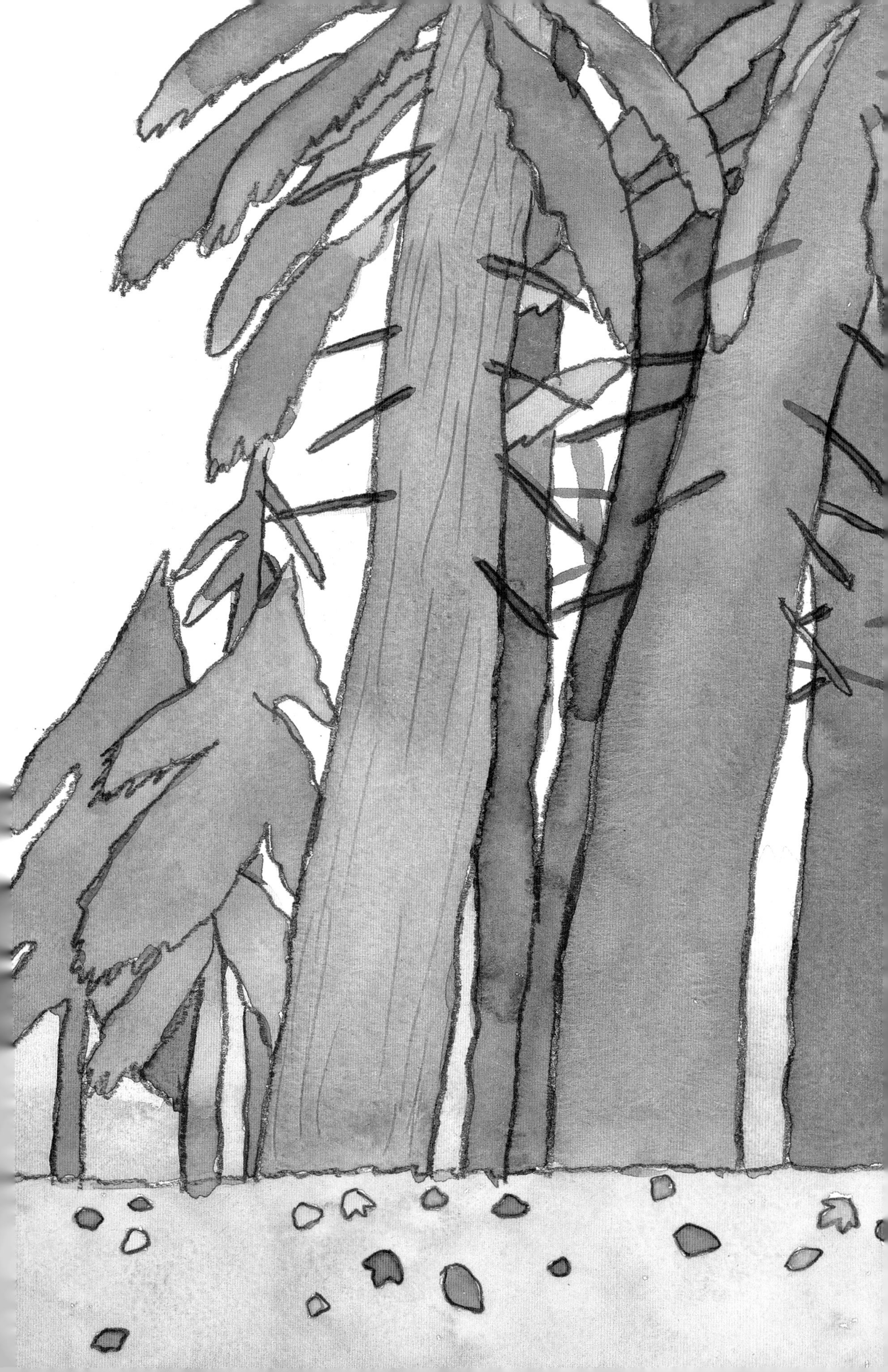

At dinner, as a reminder to stay away
from humans, Benny got only one
piece of the honey and hazelnut cake.

Mother Bear also said Benny Bear was not allowed outside of their garden for a whole week.

Benny Bear was very bored being stuck in the garden for days and days. He saw some vines and got an idea.

Using the vines, he made a very good trampoline.
He asked his sister to jump with him.

The next day Benny Bear saw his mother's yarn and remembered the fishing net. He spent the day making one.

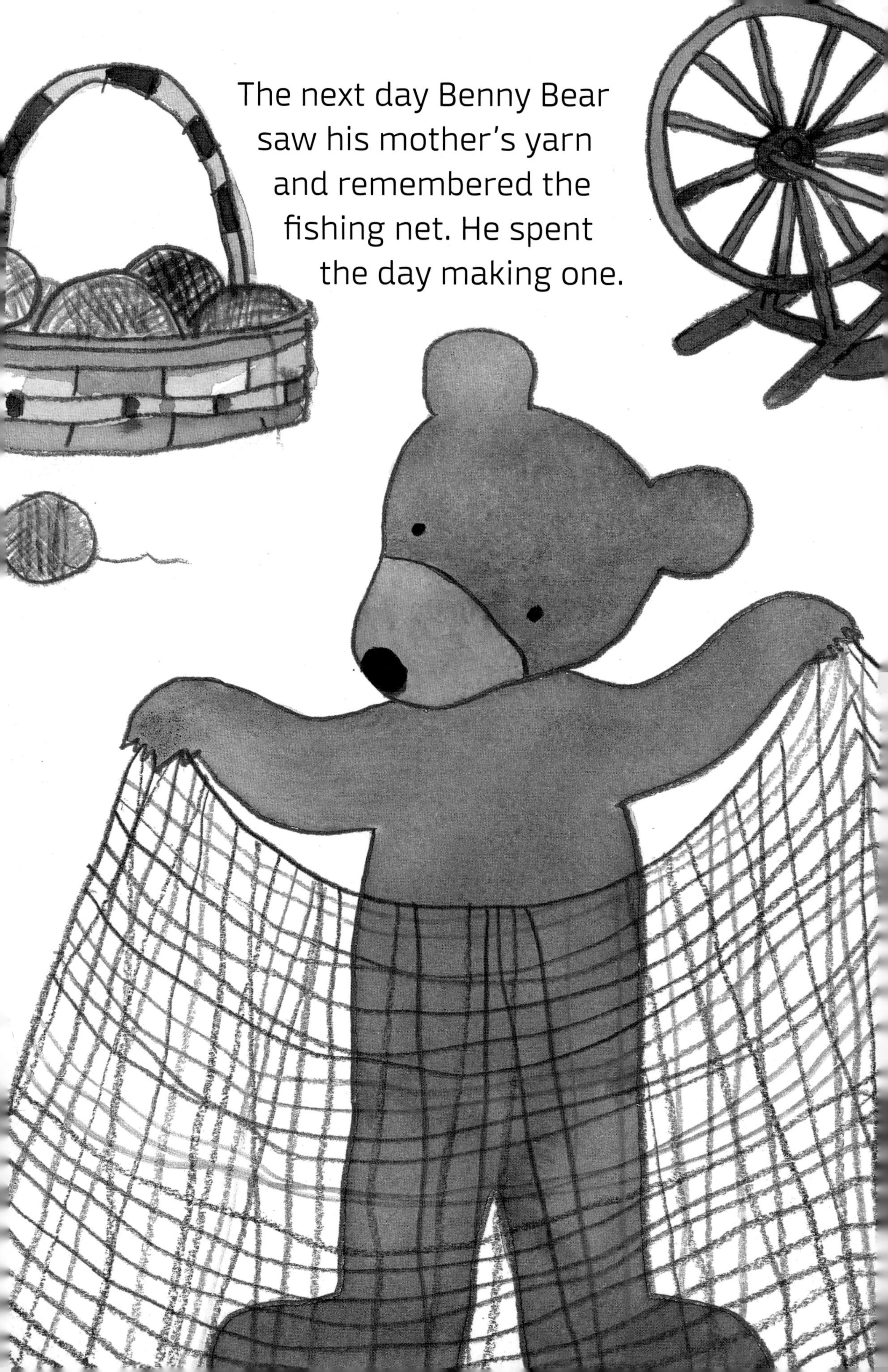

When Mother Bear finally let Benny Bear play outside the garden, he went fishing with his fishing net. It worked and he caught many fish!

Benny Bear brought the fish
home for Mother Bear to cook.

Benny Bear was happy. He had learned many lessons.

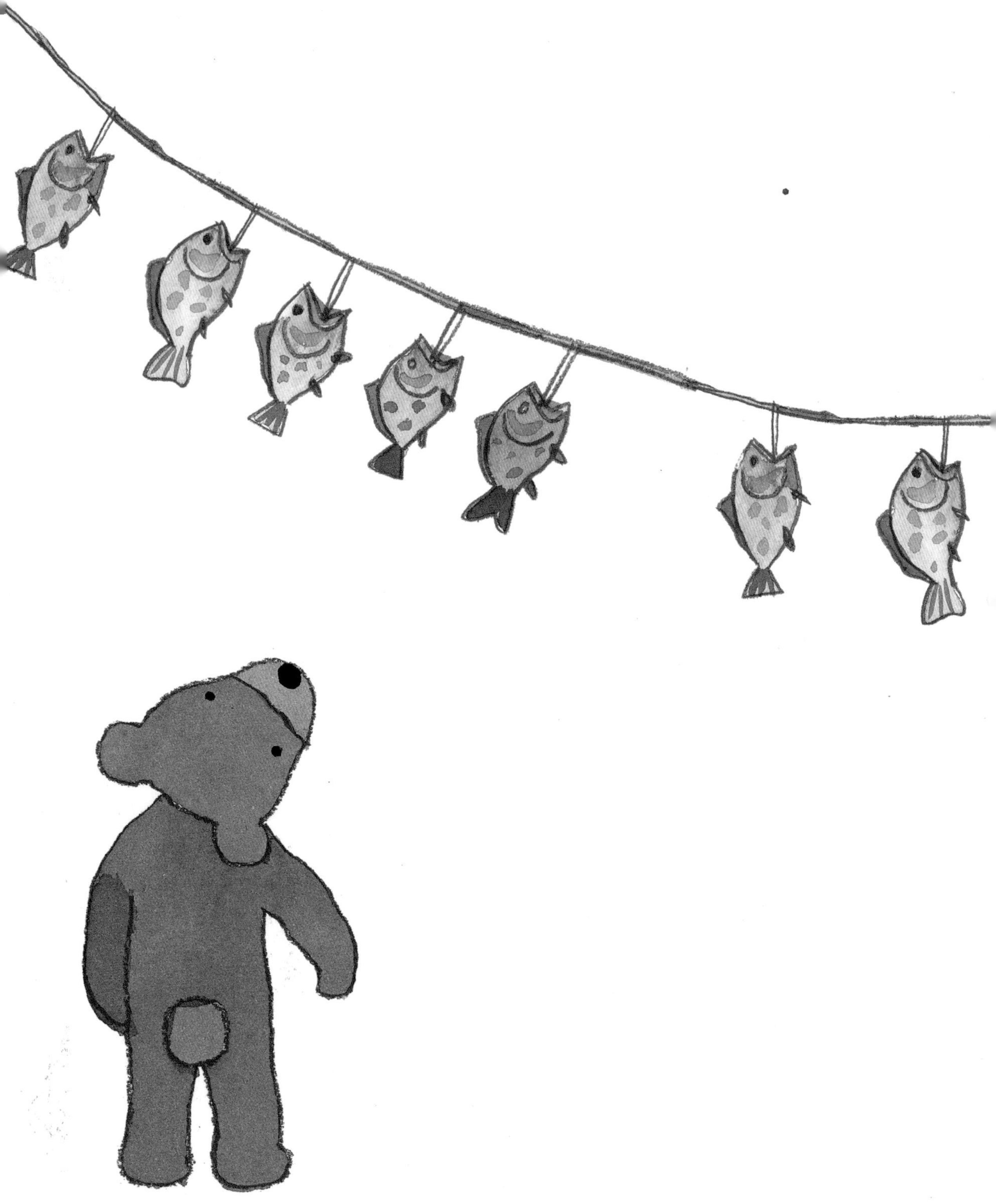